Jacques

XOXOXO

Kristin Parkinson Peabody

Jacques

by Kristen Parkinson Peabody

DORRANCE
PUBLISHING CO
EST. 1920
PITTSBURGH, PENNSYLVANIA 15238

Dorrance Publishing Co
585 Alpha Drive
Pittsburgh, PA 15238
Visit our website at *www.dorrancebookstore.com*

ISBN: 978-1-4809-4534-0
eISBN: 978-1-4809-4511-1

Jacques

On a cold, wintry day in December, a family traveling from Pennsylvania to Ohio to visit friends stopped at a rest stop along the Ohio Turnpike. Mom needed a coffee. Dad needed to stretch his legs. The children, Olivia and Mason, needed a snack. Upon opening the door to the rest stop, the family was immediately hit with the smell of freshly popped popcorn. "Do you smell that?" Olivia asked.

"Smell what?" Daddy replied jokingly.

"The delicious popcorn," Mason chimed in.

"I smell it," Mommy said with a smile. Olivia and Mason grabbed their parents' hands and led them briskly to the line for popcorn.

"Pretty please, pretty please," the children begged.

"You both know we never turn down requests for popcorn," Mommy said, laughing. After filling their bellies with fresh popcorn and drink, the children spotted a claw machine by the entrance to the rest stop.

Olivia and Mason pointed to the large red claw machine filled with stuffed animals. "Daddy, Daddy, do you have a dollar?" the children asked. Dad reached in his pocket and pulled out a crisp $1.00 bill. "Will you play for us?" Olivia asked.

"Yes," said Dad. Olivia and Mason grabbed Daddy by the hands and pulled him with excitement over to the claw machine. Mommy followed closely behind, watching the fur of Olivia's boots bounce as she moved and the red lights in Mason's boots shine with each step. Olivia and Mason looked in the claw machine. It was filled with lots of stuffed animals. One toy stood out to the children. It was a fluffy, orange monkey with a long face and large eyes.

The monkey had white accents to the ears, palms of hands, bottoms of feet and snout. "Daddy, please win us the monkey!" the children said with excitement.

Dad put the crisp $1.00 bill into the claw machine. The claw machine lit up and the timer began. Dad touched the lever and began moving the claw, lining it up carefully above the orange monkey. He looked over at Olivia and said, "Press the button." Olivia pressed the button and the claw dropped. The three metallic prongs of the claw wrapped around the orange monkey and slowly lifted up. The children looked on with excitement as the orange monkey was lifted into the air and moved to the drop area. Daddy had done it. He won the orange monkey for Olivia and Mason.

"Hooray!"

squealed the children.

Olivia removed the monkey from the claw machine. She looked him over carefully with her big, blue eyes. The monkey was soft and the fur tickled her skin. Mason looked on with wonder in his blue eyes.

Olivia handed the monkey to Mason. "Here, buddy," she said. "I want you to have him." Mason was overjoyed! He hugged the orange monkey tightly.

"What will you call your monkey?" Mommy asked.

"Jacques!" exclaimed Mason.

"Welcome to the family, Jacques," said Mommy.

Dad, Mom, Olivia, Mason and Jacques left the rest

stop together and continued on their journey.

The car ride to Cincinnati was long and snowy. Dad quietly focused on the road. Mom sang along with the radio. Olivia read a book. Mason held Jacques close. Jacques was warm and safe in Mason's arms. From that moment on, Mason knew he had found his best friend and Jacques his for-ever home.

CPSIA information can be obtained
at www.ICGtesting.com
Printed in the USA
LVHW01n1522060218
565496LV00013B/329/P